For the Rainy Lake writers,
who know what writers want

P. R.

For Pat,
in memory of Paddy

J. B.

First published 1998 by
Walker Books Ltd, 87 Vauxhall Walk
London SE11 5HJ

This edition published 1999

2 4 6 8 10 9 7 5 3 1

This book has been typeset in Cochin.

Printed in Hong Kong

British Library Cataloguing
in Publication Data
A catalogue record for this book is
available from the British Library.

ISBN 0-7445-6962-1

THIS WALKER BOOK BELONGS TO:

_____

_____

_____

_____

What Baby Wants

Phyllis Root

illustrated by Jill Barton

WALKER BOOKS
AND SUBSIDIARIES
LONDON • BOSTON • SYDNEY

Mama was tired,
but Baby wouldn't sleep.

"Don't worry," said
Grandma and Grandpa
and Aunt and Uncle
and Big Sister and
Little Brother.
"We'll take care of
Baby for you."

So Mama fed Baby,
tucked him in his cradle,
and went to bed.

WAAAAAH! said Baby.

"I know what Baby wants!"
said Grandma.
"Baby wants something
pretty to look at."

So Grandma went out to the meadow

and brought Baby an armload of flowers.
Was that what Baby wanted?

Pikala, pokala, the flowers prickled Baby's nose.

WAAAAAH! said Baby.

"I know what Baby wants!"
said Grandpa.
"Baby wants something
soft to cuddle."

So Grandpa went out to the farmyard

and brought Baby a soft feathery goose.
Was that what Baby wanted?

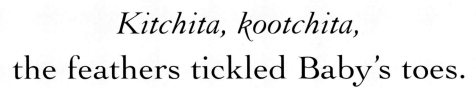

Kitchita, kootchita,
the feathers tickled Baby's toes.

WAAAAAH! said Baby.

"I know what Baby wants!" said Aunt.
"Baby wants a great big kiss."

So Aunt went out to the field

and brought Baby a cow to kiss him
with her long tongue.
Was that what Baby wanted?

Slurpilla, sloppilla,
the cow slobbered
on Baby's chin.

WAAAAAH! said Baby.

"I know what Baby wants!"
said Uncle.
"Baby wants something
to keep him warm."

So Uncle went out to the pasture

and brought Baby a flock of woolly sheep.
Was that what Baby wanted?

Nibbitty, nubbitty,
the sheep nibbled on Baby's hair.

WAAAAAH! said Baby.

"I know what Baby wants!"
said Big Sister.
"Baby wants someone
to sing him to sleep."

So Big Sister went out to the forest

and brought Baby a tree full of birds.
Was that what Baby wanted?

Tawitta, taweeta, the birds
twittered in Baby's ear.

WAAAAAH! said Baby.
WAAAAAH! WAAAAAH!
WAAAAAH!

"Oh, dear," said Grandma and Grandpa
and Aunt and Uncle and Big Sister.
"What *does* Baby want?"

"I think I know what Baby wants,"
said Little Brother.

Little Brother picked Baby up.
He cuddled Baby

and kissed Baby.

He wrapped Baby in his quilt and
sang Baby a soft little lullaby.

Was that what Baby wanted?

Hushabye, shushabye,
Baby's eyes closed.
Baby's crying
stopped.

Just then Papa came home.
"Is everything all right?" he asked.
"Just fine," said Grandma and
Grandpa and Aunt and Uncle
and Big Sister and Little Brother.
"Mama's sleeping, and we're
taking care of Baby."

And they did,
all night long.

MORE WALKER PAPERBACKS
For You to Enjoy

MRS POTTER'S PIG
by Phyllis Root / Russell Ayto

Everything in Mrs Potter's house is spotlessly clean – except for baby Ermajean.
She's always in a mess. "You'll turn into a little pig someday," Mrs Potter warns her.
And, one day, it appears that she does!

"Toddlers and older children, amused by the mess babies make,
will enjoy this story as it spills out." *The Observer*

0-7445-5262-1   £4.99

BABY DUCK
by Amy Hest / Jill Barton

Baby Duck knows what she likes and what she doesn't like.
She hates the rain and her new eyeglassses – and she's not at all keen
on the new baby either. Mother and Father Duck can't understand it.
But Grandpa can and he knows how to make Baby happy!

"Brilliant combination of text and pictures…
A night after night book for two to four-year-olds." *The Sunday Telegraph*

In the Rain with Baby Duck   0-7445-5234-6   £4.99
Baby Duck and the New Eyeglasses   0-7445-5220-6   £4.99
You're the Boss, Baby Duck!   0-7445-6305-4   £4.99

Walker Paperbacks are available from most booksellers, or by post from B.B.C.S., P.O. Box 941, Hull, North Humberside HU1 3YQ

24 hour telephone credit card line 01482 224626

To order, send: Title, author, ISBN number and price for each book ordered, your full name and address, cheque or
postal order payable to BBCS for the total amount and allow the following for postage and packing:
UK and BFPO: £1.00 for the first book, and 50p for each additional book to a maximum of £3.50.
Overseas and Eire: £2.00 for the first book, £1.00 for the second and 50p for each additional book.

Prices and availability are subject to change without notice.